LET'S CELEBRATE AMERICA

ELLIS ISLAND

Gateway to America

by Joanne Mattern

RED
CHAIR
·PRESS·

Let's Celebrate America is produced and published by Red Chair Press:
Red Chair Press LLC   PO Box 333   South Egremont, MA 01258-0333
www.redchairpress.com

About the Author

Joanne Mattern is a former editor and the author of nearly 350 books for children and teens. She began writing when she was a little girl and just never stopped! Joanne loves nonfiction because she enjoys bringing history and science topics to life and showing young readers that nonfiction is full of compelling stories! Joanne lives in New York State with her husband, four children, and several pets.

Publisher's Cataloging-In-Publication Data
Names: Mattern, Joanne, 1963–
Title: Ellis Island : gateway to America / by Joanne Mattern.

Description: South Egremont, MA : Red Chair Press, [2017] | Series: Let's celebrate America
    | Interest age level: 008-012. | Includes a glossary and references for additional reading.
    | "Core content classroom."--Cover. | Includes bibliographical references and index. |
    Summary: "For millions of people, leaving home and coming to America meant giving
    up family and all things familiar. For more than sixty years, one site was the first place in
    America all new immigrants saw. Find out why Ellis Island holds such an important place
    in America's history."--Provided by publisher.

Identifiers: LCCN 2016954995 | ISBN 978-1-63440-222-4 (library hardcover) | ISBN 978-1-63440-
    232-3 (paperback) | ISBN 978-1-63440-242-2 (ebook)

Subjects: LCSH: Ellis Island Immigration Station (N.Y. and N.J.)--History--Juvenile literature.
    | United States--Emigration and immigration--History--Juvenile literature. | CYAC: Ellis
    Island Immigration Station (N.Y. and N.J.)--History. | United States--Emigration and
    immigration--History.

Classification: LCC JV6484 .M38 2017 (print) | LCC JV6484 (ebook) | DDC 325.73--dc23

Map illustration by Joe LeMonnier

Photo credits: p. 5, 30, 31: Jeff Dinardo; p. 4, 6, 14, 15, 16, 17, 19, 20, 21, 22, 23, 24, 25, 26, 29:
Library of Congress; p. 12, 13: National Park Service; cover, p. 1, 3, 8, 9, 11, 13, 17, 18, 22, 27, 28,
back cover: Shutterstock

Printed in the United States of America
0517 1P WRZF17

Table of Contents

Gateway to America

Imagine leaving the only home you have ever known. You get on the biggest boat you have ever seen. For weeks, you live on that boat as you travel across the ocean, seeing nothing but water.

A Russian family aboard a steamship headed to America.

The steamship Prinzess Irene arriving in New York.

Finally, you hear people calling, "Land!" Everyone is excited. You rush up onto the ship's deck and see the shore. Many tall buildings stand along the water. But your eyes are fixed on a large stone and brick building right in front of you. You have arrived at Ellis Island, the Gateway to America. Over the next few hours, you will be poked and prodded. People will ask you many questions. Finally, if you are lucky, you will be free to go. You are in America now. And whether you are alone or with your family, you know this is the start of a brand new life.

For millions of Americans between 1892 and 1954, Ellis Island was the first thing they saw when they came to America. This building was a place of many hopes and dreams. It is an important part of American history.

IT'S A FACT

Almost 40 percent of Americans today had at least one ancestor pass through Ellis Island.

Sam Ellis and His Island

Before the **immigrants** came, Ellis Island was just a tiny strip of mud and clay a mile south of New York City. Native Americans called it "Gull Island" because seagulls nested there. In 1634, Native Americans sold Gull Island to the Dutch West India Company. The island had several owners after that. Finally, in 1775, a British merchant named Samuel Ellis bought the island. He named the island after himself. Sam Ellis caught fish and oysters in the waters around the island.

Ellis Island today.

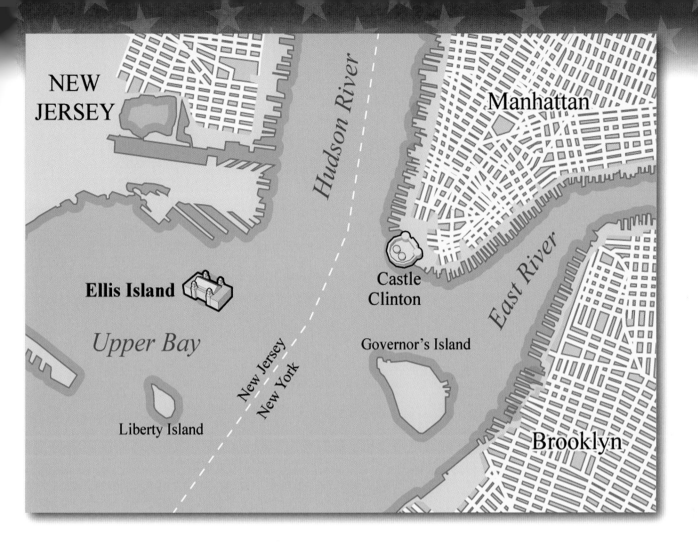

In 1785, Sam Ellis moved to New Jersey. A few years later, he gave the U.S. government permission to build a fort on his island. After Sam Ellis died the island was sold to New York State. Finally, in 1810, New York State sold the island to the U.S. government.

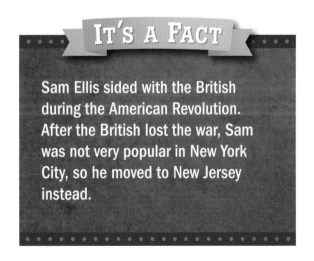

IT'S A FACT

Sam Ellis sided with the British during the American Revolution. After the British lost the war, Sam was not very popular in New York City, so he moved to New Jersey instead.

Fort Gibson

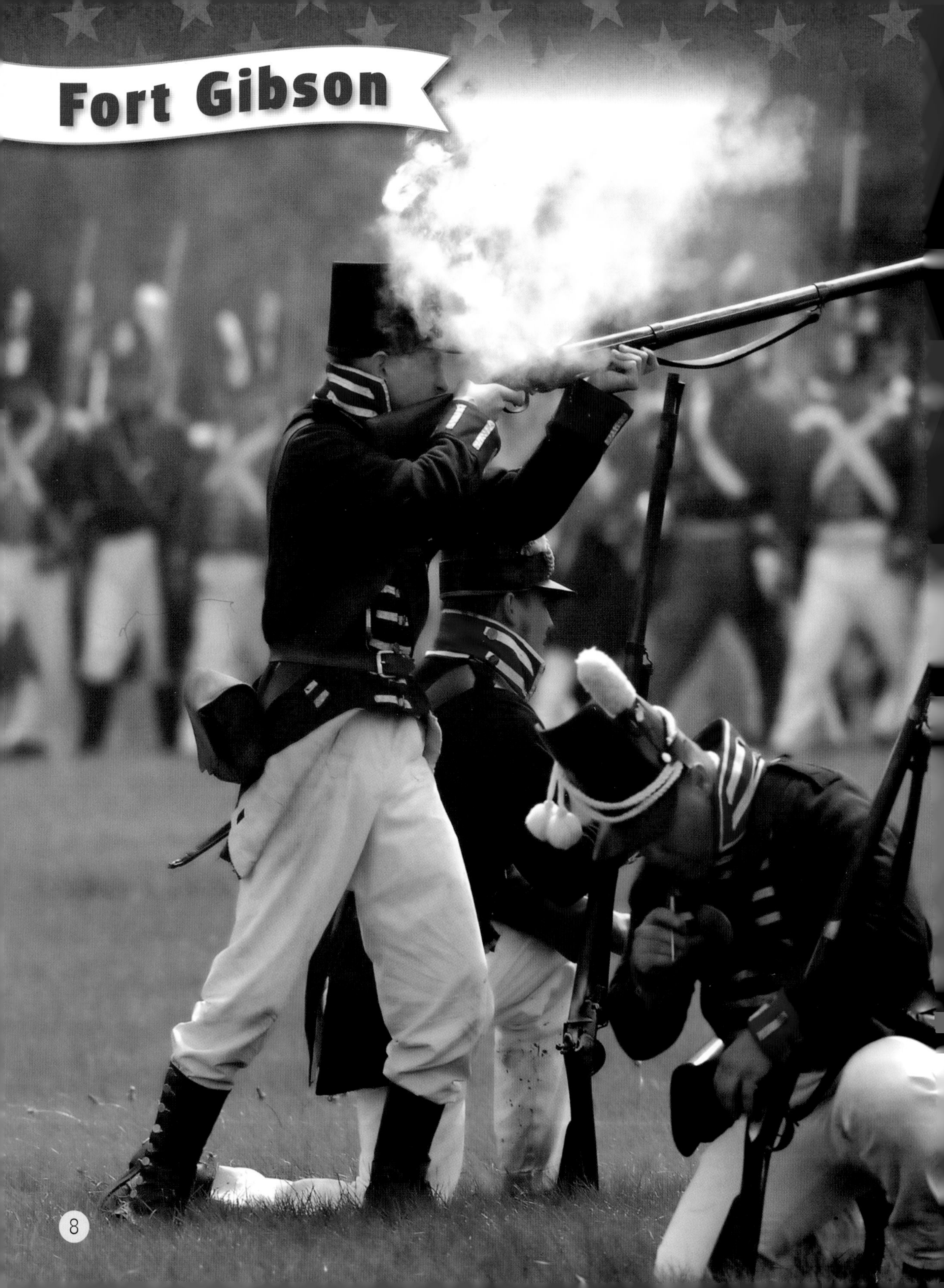

As soon as the United States bought the land, they built a fort on it. The fort was one of many built on islands around New York City to protect the city from British attacks during the War of 1812.

After the War of 1812 ended, the fort was renamed Fort Gibson to honor two American officers killed during the war. In 1843, the government used Fort Gibson to store ammunition and explosives. The people who lived in New York City and nearby New Jersey weren't very happy about that! In spite of the danger, those explosives remained on the island for another fifty years.

War of 1812

In under 30 years after the American Revolution ended, the United States and Britain were at war again. On June 18, 1812, the U.S. Congress declared war on Britain claiming Britain was interfering with the new nation's international relations and trade. By September 1814, British ships began returning home. The young nation had survived its first important challenge.

An American gun crew prepares to fire during a War of 1812 reenactment.

The Original Immigration Station

During the 1840s, many people began to immigrate to the United States. There were many wars fought in Europe during this time, and many economic and political challenges. Thousands of people decided that starting a new life in the United States was the best solution to their problems.

Until 1855, anyone could enter the United States as long as a doctor stated the person was healthy. There was no system to greet immigrants or help them get settled in their new land. This caused a lot of problems and many immigrants were cheated or abused. New York State decided that it would be better to have all immigrants pass through one central station so they could receive services and safely find their relatives. The state made Castle Clinton, a fort in lower Manhattan, into a new immigration station. This station was called Castle Garden.

IT'S A FACT

Until 1855, a doctor rowed out to every ship in New York Harbor to check the health of the passengers and crew on board.

Immigrants leaving a steamship at Castle Garden in 1884.

The Castle Garden immigration station opened on August 1, 1855. Both immigrants and the city of New York benefited from the new station. Immigrants received medical exams there. They could book tickets to other cities in the United States or find housing in the city if they wished to stay. Castle Garden had food stands, clean bathrooms, and an area where immigrants could meet their relatives.

Having all immigrants go through one central station also allowed New York to inspect each immigrant. Officials made sure no one had any serious diseases or a criminal record.

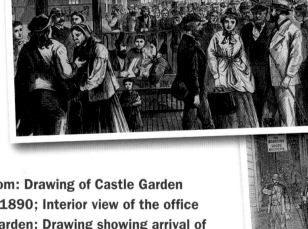

Top to bottom: Drawing of Castle Garden complex in 1890; Interior view of the office at Castle Garden; Drawing showing arrival of immigrants at Castle Garden in 1866.

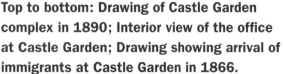

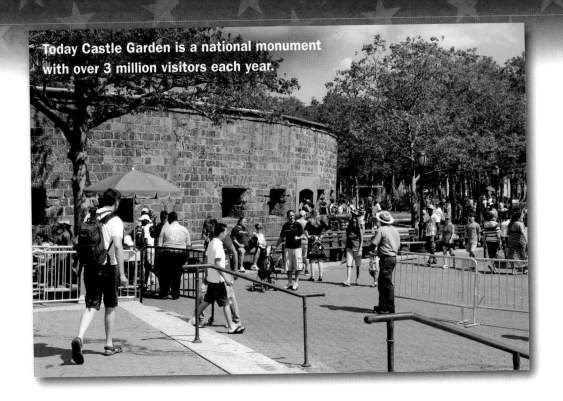
Today Castle Garden is a national monument with over 3 million visitors each year.

By 1890, the number of immigrants flowing into America had increased tremendously. Americans wanted stricter laws. They worried about the people who flooded into the country. Also, there were many problems at Castle Garden. Dishonest people took advantage of immigrants. Finally, the U.S. government got involved. It decided that a larger, more modern inspection station had to be built to solve all the problems. That new station would be located on Ellis Island.

IT'S A FACT

Before it was an immigration station, Castle Garden was used as a theater and opera house.

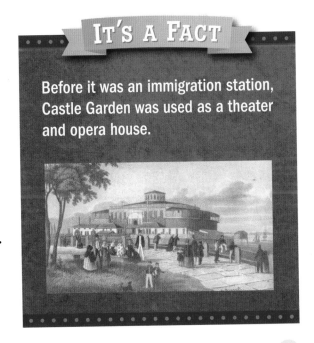

The New Immigration Station

In 1890, all the explosives were removed from Ellis Island. Workers also made the island bigger by dumping boatloads of soil around its shores. They put up new buildings on the island. The most important was the Registry Building. This building opened on January 1, 1892 and began processing immigrants.

Conditions were often crowded on the boats.

Newly arrived Italian immigrants.

In 1897, a terrible fire broke out on Ellis Island. Because the buildings were made of wood, all of them were destroyed. The U.S. government quickly rebuilt the station. All the new buildings were made of stone, brick, and concrete so they were fireproof. In December 1900, the new station opened—just in time for a fresh new wave of immigration.

During the peak years of American immigration—1892 through 1932—more than 12 million people from around the world immigrated to America through Ellis Island. In the year 1907 alone, 1,004,756 new arrivals were processed in the new Ellis Island station.

Immigrants inside the station, waiting to be processed.

15

The Medical Exam

All ships entering New York Harbor stopped at a **quarantine** station about six miles from the city. Health inspectors boarded the ship and checked for **contagious** diseases. Anyone who was sick was sent to a hospital on another island. Finally, all the first-class and second-class passengers were allowed to leave the ship. However, things were different for most of the immigrants, who traveled in third class, or **steerage**. These passengers paid the cheapest fares and lived in the poorest conditions on the ship.

Immigrants waiting for medical inspections.

Most immigrants brought whatever they could carry with them since they were not planning to return home. They packed everything from quilts and clothing to favorite dolls and valuable items like musical instruments and samovars for brewing tea. They carried their possessions in trunks, suitcases, baskets, boxes and sometimes just bundled together with rope or string.

Some immigrants brought items from home such as this samovar.

Third-class immigrants arrived at Ellis Island from the ship on small ferryboats. Once on the island, they were told to leave their baggage in a storage room. Then immigrants walked up a long, steep flight of stairs. Doctors watched them from the top of the stairs. They looked for anyone who had trouble walking, seeing, or breathing. These immigrants were immediately pulled out of line for medical tests. Everyone else was examined by two doctors.

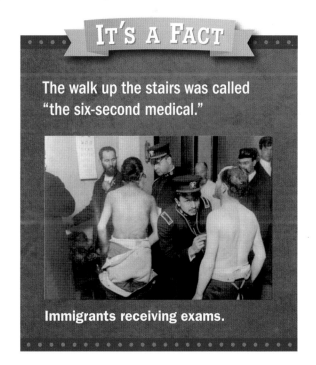

IT'S A FACT

The walk up the stairs was called "the six-second medical."

Immigrants receiving exams.

17

Off a Ferry and Into History

When Annie Moore, a 15-year-old Irish girl, walked off a ferryboat on January 1, 1892, she made history by becoming the first immigrant processed at the newly opened Ellis Island Immigration Center. Annie had come over with her two younger brothers to join their parents in New York. To mark the historical moment, Immigration Officials presented Annie with a 10-dollar gold piece. Over the next thirty years, 12 million people followed in Annie's footsteps. For all of them, Ellis Island was more than just a processing center, it was a place that marked the start of the rest of their lives, or dashed their dreams by sending them back to their homelands. For all of them, it would be remembered as either the Isle of Hope or the Isle of Tears.

The first doctor made sure immigrants could walk, hear, see, and speak. They looked for any obvious physical or mental problems. The second doctor checked the immigrants' eyes. He used a metal hook to roll back an immigrant's eyelid to check for a disease called trachoma. If a doctor thought an immigrant had a medical problem, he marked the immigrant's coat with chalk. These immigrants went to a private room to be checked more completely.

Statues of Annie and her brothers stand in both Ellis Island and County Cork, Ireland.

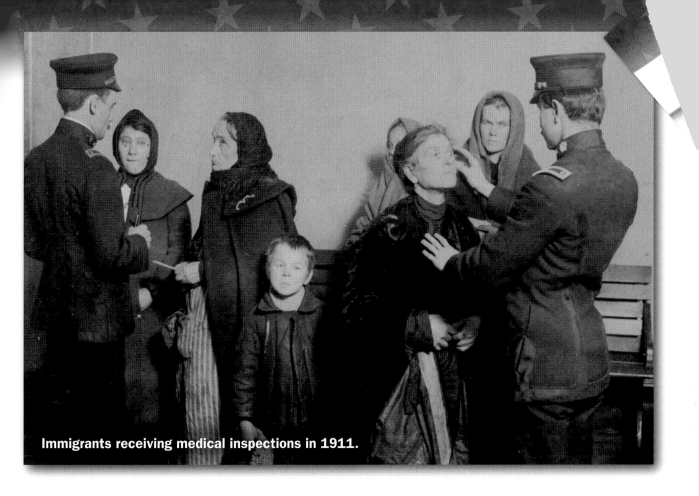
Immigrants receiving medical inspections in 1911.

If an immigrant had a serious medical problem, such as tuberculosis or trachoma, he or she was **deported**, or sent back home. Immigrants who could be cured spent time in a hospital on the island. Sometimes families were split up because one member was sick while the others were healthy.

While only 2% of Ellis Island arrivals were actually deported, everyone feared the possibility. The U.S. government had an agreement with the steamship companies that were carrying immigrants to America. If any person was refused entry into the U.S., the companies had agreed to take the person home for free.

Stuck on the Island

After passing the medical exams, immigrants faced a legal exam. One by one, they stood before an inspector and stated their name, place of birth, occupation, and if they had relatives living in America. Inspectors usually spent just a few minutes with each immigrant. Most immigrants passed the exam and were allowed to enter the United States. They made their way into New York City or bought a railroad ticket to travel somewhere else in America. Immigrants sent telegrams or letters, had something to eat, and waited for relatives to pick them up.

Not everyone left the island. Some immigrants had to stay because of medical or legal problems. Others had to wait for a relative to pick them up or wait for a sick family member to leave the Ellis Island hospital. These immigrants stayed in dormitories on the island. Men and women slept in separate rooms. Children usually stayed with their mothers. There was a dining room where immigrants could eat and areas where immigrant children could play.

IT'S A FACT

Immigrants arrived from all over the world. But mostly they came from these countries:

- Italy
- Hungary
- Russia
- Germany
- Britain
- Ireland
- Sweden
- Canada

What's Your Name?

Though it seems like an easy enough question, many of the inspectors could not understand the immigrants' accents. As a result, they spelled names as they sounded. In one example, a German-speaking Jewish immigrant named Isaac was so nervous when asked his name that he replied "Vergessen" which means "I forget" in German. Not understanding his reply, the immigration inspector wrote down "Isaac Ferguson." Many immigrants were afraid to correct the misspellings of their names, so their official documents gave them new names or spellings.

An inspector questions new arrivals to verify information.

Changes on the Island

In 1914, fewer than 900,000 immigrants entered the United States through Ellis Island. Then World War I broke out in Europe. It became difficult for immigrants to travel overseas. By 1918, when the war finally ended, the number of immigrants passing through Ellis Island had dropped to under 28,000.

Immigration picked up again after the war ended, but the United States government began to restrict immigration. The government created **quotas**, or limits on how many people could enter the United States from other countries.

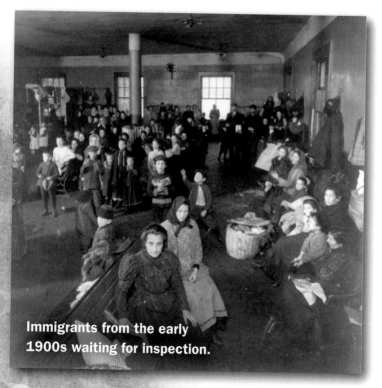

Immigrants from the early 1900s waiting for inspection.

After new laws passed, immigration became more controlled.

Laws changed in other ways. The Immigration Act of 1924 required immigrants to pass medical and legal inspections in their home countries before travelling to the U.S. Immigrants who passed these tests and met the quota were given **visas** and could enter the United States right away. They did not need to be inspected at Ellis Island. By 1932, only 3,000 people were admitted through Ellis Island station.

IT'S A FACT

Many immigrants were surprised at the food served in the Ellis Island dining room. Many had never seen bananas before and had to be shown how to peel them.

After 1932, most of the people at Ellis Island were waiting to be deported back to their home countries. The island became a prison instead of a gateway to a new life. After the United States entered World War II in 1941, thousands of soldiers were trained on Ellis Island. Some buildings on the island were used as hospitals for wounded soldiers.

Immigrants who were deemed undesirable waited in detention pens like this to be returned to their home countries.

Aerial view of Ellis Island from the early 1900s.

About 6,000–7,000 German, Japanese, and Italian people living in America were classified as **enemy aliens**. The government worried that they would aid the countries we were fighting against. These people were sent to Ellis Island while their cases went through the court system. Officials on the island tried to make their stay as pleasant as possible. Enemy aliens had visitors and could make phone calls. They were served ethnic food and given areas where they could play sports and games. But, still they were being held against their wishes.

After World War II, immigrants began traveling to the United States by airplane. There was no longer a need for an immigration station on the island. On November 29, 1954, Ellis Island closed its doors.

Ellis Island Abandoned

After it closed, Ellis Island was abandoned. No one in the U.S. or New York State governments wanted it. In 1962, people began suggesting that Ellis Island become a **monument** to American immigration. In 1965, Ellis Island became part of the National Park Service. However, there was not enough money to **restore** the island. The buildings began to fall apart. Pipes froze, and parts of the roof collapsed. Broken glass and plaster fell on the floors. Pigeons flew in and out of the broken windows and puddles of water covered the floor.

During the 1970s, another effort began to save Ellis Island. Donations poured in from people all over the country. Finally, by 1984 there was enough money to restore the main building. On September 9, 1990, the new Ellis Island Immigration Museum finally opened to the public.

Most of the buildings were abandoned and left to the elements after the immigration station closed in 1954.

When Ellis Island closed, the New York Times wrote,

"The immigrants made their way into the texture of our national life... They make part of what is now the American temperament—a livelier and richer national personality than could have existed without them."

Ellis Island Reborn

Ellis Island quickly became a popular tourist destination. The museum is filled with exhibits documenting the immigrant journey. Visitors can see artifacts brought by immigrant families and listen to recorded oral histories. They can climb the staircase and look up records about their ancestors on computers.

Other buildings on the island still need repair. The National Park Service is working to restore these other buildings, including the hospital where many immigrants stayed. Perhaps someday in the future, visitors can experience even more of the immigrant's journey to America.

Display at the Ellis Island Museum of actual luggage left by some of the immigrants.

Just outside the main building stands a monument to all American immigrants, the Wall of Honor. Names of over 700,000 immigrants appear along this long wall. Almost every nationality is included in this list of names—an important reminder that America is a nation of immigrants.

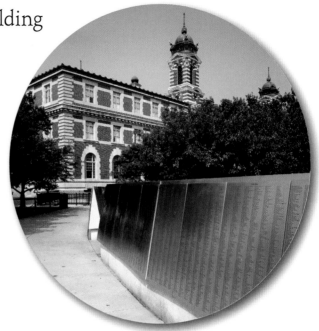

Every nationality is represented on the Wall of Honor.

More than twelve million immigrants passed through Ellis Island between 1892 and 1954. Each of them had a unique story to tell, and each of them shaped the future of our country. The immigrants who came through Ellis Island gave up everything in search of a better life. They changed America forever and added their talents and skills to our national story.

Almost everyone in the United States is descended from immigrants. Places like Ellis Island are a chance to learn about our history and experience both the beauty and challenges of coming to a new land.

Glossary

contagious: easily spread from one person to another

deported: sent back to a person's home country

enemy aliens: any native or citizen of a foreign nation which a domestic nation or government is in conflict with

immigrants: people who move from one country to live in another country

monument: a statue or building erected to commemorate a historical person or event

quarantine: a period or place of isolation for people or animals exposed to a contagious disease

quotas: laws that limit the number of people who can enter a country

restore: to return something to its former condition

steerage: the part of a ship for people paying the cheapest fares

visas: documents allowing a person to enter a country

Learn More in the Library

Books

Carney, Elizabeth. *Ellis Island* (National Geo Kids).
National Geographic Childrens' Publishing, 2016.

Demuth, Patricia Brennan. *What Was Ellis Island?*
Grosset & Dunlap, 2014.

Landau, Elaine. *Ellis Island* (True Books). Scholastic, 2008.

Web Sites

Official National Park Service site for
Ellis Island National Monument
www.nps.gov/elis/index.htm

Facts and data for America's first immigration center
www.castlegarden.org

Index